The Old Man

and the

Carole Jean Tremblay
Illustrations by Angela Donato

Pineapple Press, Inc.
Sarasota, Florida

To Jean-Paul, Alain, and Joanne
With love,
Maman

Text copyright (c) 2006 by Carole Jean Tremblay
Illustrations copyright (c) 2006 by Angela Donato

Inquiries should be addressed to:

Pineapple Press, Inc.
P.O. Box 3889
Sarasota, Florida 34230

www.pineapplepress.com

Library of Congress Cataloging-in-Publication Data

Tremblay, Carole Jean
  The old man and the C / Carole Jean Tremblay.— 1st ed.
       p. cm.
  Summary: Possessing only a small rowboat and simple fishing pole, optimistic Charlie,
the oldest fisherman on the coast, enters a fishing tournament, with unexpected results.
  ISBN-13: 978-1-56164-354-7 (hardback : alk. paper)
  ISBN-10: 1-56164-354-8 (hardback : alk. paper)
[1. Fishers—Fiction. 2. Fishing—Fiction. 3. Contests—Fiction. 4. Old age—Fiction.]   I. Title.
  PZ7.T6853Ol 2006
  [E]—dc22

                                                        2005032299

First Edition
10 9 8 7 6 5 4 3 2 1

Design by Shé Heaton
Printed in China

"Everything about him was old except his eyes and they were the same color as the sea and were cheerful and undefeated."
Ernest Hemingway, *The Old Man and the Sea*

Charlie was the oldest fisherman on the coast. To hear him tell it, he was also the smartest. No one knew exactly how old Charlie was, but with his sun-seasoned face and vegetable-brush beard, he looked like Old King Neptune himself.

Charlie's dream was to catch the biggest fish in the sea, but he didn't have a big fishing boat. He didn't have a net or harpoons. All he had was a leaky old rowboat and a fishing rod that was probably catching fish when Charlie was still a boy. He named his rowboat the *C-Worthy* because, well . . . because Charlie was an optimist.

Charlie went out to sea every day in the *C-Worthy*. He caught lots of little fish—blackfish, sheepsheads, even flying fish. But he never had any luck catching the big fish—the marlins, tarpons, and swordfish. All the big fish swam around the big boats. They got caught in the nets. They got speared by harpoons. They didn't even look at Charlie's fishline and the squishy, squirmy little worms he used for bait.

One day, Charlie saw a big poster tacked up on the door of Roger's Bait and Supply Shop.

ANNOUNCING
The FIRST Annual
FISH-OR-CUT-BAIT FISHING TOURNAMENT
Sign up here!
Prizes for: The Biggest Catch
The Longest Catch
Trophy for: The Most Unusual Catch
Open to All
Entry fee: $10

"That's it," Charlie said to himself. "I'm going to sign up right now. I'll show those big shots what a real fisherman can do. They'll see!"

On the day of the tournament, Charlie was down at the docks before the stars went to bed. He had switched his prized Brooklyn Dodgers baseball cap for his extra-lucky fisherman's hat, the one with all the pins and fishhooks. He wiped off the *C-Worthy*'s motor with an old rag torn from someone's red flannel pajamas. He tested his line. He peered into his bait pail to check on the squishy, squirmy little worms. When he was satisfied that all was well, he swung his lunch basket under the *C-Worthy*'s weathered front seat and climbed in.

One by one, the other contestants arrived at the pier. There were vacationers in rented boats, looking like fish out of water. There were city folks, fishing for compliments in their fancy yachts. There were local kids, with fishing rods made of bamboo, in old motorized row-boats like the *C-Worthy*.

"I've got more fishing know-how than all the others put together," Charlie chuckled. "I'm sure to win one of the prizes, and—why not?—maybe all three!"

Roger opened the door of his bait supply shop at six A.M. sharp. Looking very important (he had on his best Sunday T-shirt), he announced the tournament rules:

"Welcome to the First Annual Fish-Or-Cut-Bait Fishing Tournament. The rules are—no rules! Be back no later than five o'clock this afternoon for judging and a free fish-and-chips supper for all contestants. Good luck to everybody. Now get going!"

Charlie needed no encouragement. He primed the motor, pulled the cord, and BRRRRUUUGGGGG, the *C-Worthy* chugged out of the harbor. He watched over his shoulder as all the other boats turned south.

"That's what I thought!" said Charlie gleefully. "They'll all fight for the same fish. I'll go north and be all alone. I'm going to catch the biggest, longest, most unusual fish in the sea."

Charlie drank in the salty air. The sharp, briny smell seemed to foretell a lucky day. He sang out the chorus of an old sea chantey, and the *C-Worthy*'s motor kept the beat.

Two hours later, Charlie arrived at his secret fishing grounds. It was in a small deserted bay. Hundreds of mangrove trees plunged their tangled roots into the salty water. The mangroves were so thick they completely hid the bay from the shore. Charlie recognized the spot, because there were always lots of pelicans and fish hawks diving into the water to catch little fish.

"If there are lots of little fish," Charlie reasoned, "there must be big fish who come to eat the little fish. And then even bigger fish to eat them!"

Charlie cut the *C-Worthy*'s engine. He pulled a rusty iron anchor from under the bow.

"If I win this tournament, I'm going to buy a gallon of red paint and repaint this old thing, inside and out," he grumbled, as he dropped the anchor over the side of the *C-Worthy*. He watched it descend into the clear waters of the bay until it hit the sandy bottom, sending up a watery cloud of silver speckles.

Then he chose the squishiest, squirmiest little worm in his bait pail and laced it onto his hook. With a flick of his wrist, he cast his line far across the calm waters of the secret bay.

The squishy, squirmy little worm sailed past a diving pelican and landed in the water—well, almost in the water. In fact, it landed right in the mouth of a hungry little fish.

"Bravo!" cried Charlie, "Step one of my plan is a success."

Charlie pulled in his catch. In no time, he fixed the hook solidly in the mouth of the little red and blue porgy. Then he threw his line back into the sea. This time he had to wait a little longer before feeling a tug. When it came, he was ready. He hurriedly reeled in his line to find a lovely black drumfish, chomping on the little porgy.

"Step two—done!" he cried. And back into the sea went the drumfish, this time as bait instead of catch. He slipped his fishing rod into the special holder he had found in a boat junkyard. It was now clamped solidly to the side of the *C-Worthy*. The next catch might be the big one! He didn't want to lose it, or worse, be pulled out of his boat trying to hold onto it.

Again Charlie waited. He waited patiently. He waited impatiently. He munched on a piece of beef jerky. He drank a bottle of sarsaparilla. He did a crossword. And he waited. Eleven o'clock. Noon. One o'clock. Nothing. His eyes began to tire. Blinks became nods. His wrinkled chin settled into his stubby white beard. His beard scratched against his sunburnt chest. Soon he was dreaming a fisherman's dream about catching a fish so huge, so mighty, so beautiful, that only a true fisherman could imagine such a creature.

With a jerk, Charlie's line came to life. Something was biting. Something big! The *C-Worthy* began to move. Charlie could feel the anchor scraping along the sandy bottom. He grabbed his fishing rod above the holder and held on with all his might.

"This is it!" he cried out. "This is the biggest fish I ever caught. This is the biggest fish in the sea!"

The *C-Worthy* began making wild zigzags across the bay. Her wake looked like skaters' trails on a winter lake— but Charlie had never seen a frozen lake. For a moment, he thought how the white slashes in the water looked like flashes of lightning in an August afternoon sky. But the terrible fish on the end of his line didn't give him time to be poetic.

The *C-Worthy* was pulled back and forth across the bay. Back and forth swam the captured fish, thrashing through the water. If only the line could hold!

C harlie gasped as he watched the watery trail of the invisible fish turn toward the open sea. He was being pulled out of the bay. What could he do if the fish towed him far from the shore? What if the fish towed him to South America! How would he ever get back? Should he cut his line and lose the biggest fish he had ever caught?

Suddenly, the *C-Worthy* jerked to a halt, sending Charlie crashing to his knees. At the same instant, the maddened fish leaped into the air, like a charging dog suddenly arriving at the end of its leash. Charlie was so busy fighting to keep his balance, he didn't get a good look at his catch.

"The anchor must be caught on a rock! Oh, please let it hold tight. Please!" Charlie begged.

The *C-Worthy* creaked and cracked, pulled forward by the fish and held back by the anchor. All the while, Charlie tried to steady his arms as the boat rocked to and fro. He knew he must be careful not to lose his catch. Now it was his intelligence and skill against the strength and endurance of the great fish. He pulled back on his fishing rod. Then with a quick forward movement, he relaxed the rod and reeled in some line. Next, he let out a little line so his rod wouldn't break. Then he pulled it back, relaxed, and again quickly reeled in some line. His old arms began to ache from the effort. His wrinkled knees pressed hard against the side of the rowboat.

Charlie tried to see the fish through the churning waters. He squinted his sky-blue eyes under his faded green fisherman's hat. Little by little, he pulled the big fish in toward the *C-Worthy*. Finally he could see the wild creature on the end of his line. It was a blue marlin.

"What a fish! He must be twelve feet long!" marveled Charlie. "He must weigh four hundred pounds!"

The battle lasted for two hours. Who would give up first, the fish or Charlie? The marlin tore and spluttered and gnashed his great teeth. Suddenly, he came close alongside the *C-Worthy*.

He looked up at Charlie and said, "HIC!"

What was that? "HIC!" There it goes again! "HIC! HIC!" Charlie's arms fell to his sides. His jaw dropped open. He couldn't believe his ears. The marlin had the hiccups!

The marlin heaved a final horrendous "HICCUP!" and out of his mouth and into the rowboat tumbled a dark, roundish object. The fishhook followed, and the marlin realized that he was free. With a last little "HIC!" he did a back dive away from the *C-Worthy* and swam out to sea.

"What can I do now?" Charlie wailed. "No fish, no prize, no trophy. How can I face going back to the fishing pier today? Everyone will make fun of me."

Charlie slumped down onto the *C-Worthy*'s worn wooden seat. He fished his red-checkered handkerchief out of his pocket and wiped his reddened eyes.

And then he saw it. It looked like an old cast-off horseshoe, covered with seaweed and muck. Charlie suddenly remembered that the marlin had spit something out just before getting away. Probably something he ate before taking Charlie's bait.

"I can't be bothered with that now," thought Charlie. "I've got other fish to fry. Actually," he corrected himself, "I don't have a single fish to fry!"

Charlie pushed away the object with the toe of his weathered fisherman's boot. It scraped across the bottom of the rowboat. Despite his discouragement, he was curious. He bent down and picked up the strange object. It was very heavy. Pouah! It smelled of rotting seaweed. Charlie held it over the *C-Worthy*'s side and swished it through the water. Then he fished an old rag out of his tackle box and began wiping. As he wiped, his unbelieving eyes widened.

What was this thing that began to shine with a warm yellow glow? He cleaned and polished, polished and cleaned. Soon he realized the object was in the form of a letter—a C, a golden C. Charlie was holding a golden treasure!

"I've heard of fishing for sunken treasure, but this is simply fishy! Where did this C-thing come from?" Charlie asked himself. "How did it get into the marlin's throat? And what is the C for, anyway? Not Charlie! . . . Maybe Columbus? . . . Maybe Cortez! . . . It must be worth a fortune!" Charlie whispered, afraid to believe his luck. Carefully, he wrapped his treasure in some fishy-smelling newspaper and stowed it under the seat.

But then he remembered the contest.

"What can I do with a C, even a golden C?" Charlie said out loud, "I don't have a chance of winning the tournament. I don't have a single fish to show."

Charlie slowly maneuvered the *C-Worthy* around to free the anchor. He pulled on the frayed engine cord.

"Come on, old girl, let's go back and face the music." And ZOOM, ZOOM, the *C-Worthy* lurched forward, as if trying her best to deserve her name.

At four fifty-five, Charlie threw out his dock line to Billy Fisher. Billy tied the *C-Worthy* to the pier. Charlie climbed up the rope ladder and shuffled over to the bait shop, his stiff old legs wobbling at each step.

He saw Ben Whalen standing proudly next to a huge tarpon, suspended on the fish scale. The needle marked 255 pounds! And Annie Poisson was explaining excitedly, to everyone who would listen, how she had caught the superb sailfish her crew was hoisting onto the pier.

"Hey, Charlie, where's your fish?" Roger cried out.

"Well, I don't really know now!" Charlie muttered.

"Yeah, sure," teased Billy Fisher, "I bet you're going to make us all cry with a sob story about the one that got away."

"One did get away," Charlie protested, "a giant marlin. I fought with him for two hours before bringing him alongside the *C-Worthy*. Then, just as I was about to pull him in, he got the hiccups."

"Aw, come on, Charlie," drawled Danny Dupont. "Don't go makin' up any cockamamie excuses 'bout why you didn't win the tournament."

"I know I didn't win, Danny. Don't rub it in. But I did catch something interesting. Look!"

As the other fishermen looked on in amazement, he unwrapped the golden C.

"Wwwhew!" Annie whistled.

"That thing must be as old as you are, Charlie!" Roger teased. "But you can't win a prize with that C, Charlie. It's not the longest fish. Annie's is longer. It's not the biggest fish. Ben's is heavier. And, I admit your C is very unusual, but it's *not* a fish!"

"Of course it's not a fish. I never said it was a fish!" Charlie snapped, looking away from Roger's mocking face.

Just then, Charlie's gaze rested on the poster tacked up on the bait shop door. Trying to look unconcerned, he read and reread the tournament rules. Suddenly, his eyes lit up. His bushy eyebrows arched. His mouth opened and closed excitedly above his vegetable-brush beard.

"Stop!" he cried. "Look! Look at the poster! It doesn't say the most unusual *fish*. It says the most unusual *catch*. I caught the C! I win the trophy!"

Billy Fisher guffawed. Ben and Annie cheered. Charlie beamed.

And Roger vowed that next year, the poster wouldn't say most unusual "catch." Next year, it would say FISH!

If you enjoyed reading this book, here are some other Pineapple Press titles you might enjoy as well. To request our complete catalog or to place an order, write to Pineapple Press, P.O. Box 3889, Sarasota, Florida 34230, or call 1-800-PINEAPL (746-3275). Or visit our website at www.pineapplepress.com.

Those Amazing Alligators by Kathy Feeney. Illustrated by Steve Weaver. Alligators are amazing animals, as you'll see in this book. Discover the differences between alligators and crocodiles; learn what alligators eat, how they communicate, and much more. Ages 5–9.

Those Outrageous Owls by Laura Wyatt. Illustrated by Steve Weaver, photographs by H. G. Moore III. Learn what owls eat, how they hunt, and why they look the way they do. You'll find out what an owlet looks like, why horned owls have horns, and much more! Ages 5–9.

Those Terrific Turtles by Sarah Cussen. Illustrated by Steve Weaver, photographs by David M. Dennis. This book of questions and answers will convince you that turtles are indeed terrific! You'll learn the difference between a turtle and a tortoise, and find out why they have shells. Meet baby turtles and some very, very old ones, and even explore a pond. Ages 5–9.

Those Excellent Eagles by Jan Lee Wicker. Illustrated by Steve Weaver, photographs by H.G. Moore III. Learn all about those excellent eagles—what they eat, how fast they fly, why the American Bald Eagle is our nation's national bird. You'll even make some edible eagles! Ages 5–9.

Those Peculiar Pelicans by Sarah Cussen. Illustrated by Steve Weaver, photographs by Roger Hammond. Find out how much food those peculiar pelicans can fit in their beaks, how they stay cool, whether they really steal fish from fishermen. And learn how to fold up an origami pelican. Ages 5–9.

Those Funny Flamingos by Jan Lee Wicker. Illustrated by Steve Weaver. Flamingos are indeed funny birds. Learn why those funny flamingos are pink, stand on one leg, eat upside down, and much more. Ages 5–9.

Esmeralda and the Enchanted Pond by Susan Ryan. Delightful, full-color illustrations highlight the story of Esmeralda and her father, who visit a Florida forest during all four seasons and discover that there's a scientific explanation for everything that seems magical. An illustrated activity guide that conforms to the Sunshine State Standards is also available. Ages 8–11.

The Florida Water Story by Peggy Sias Lantz and Wendy A. Hale. Illustrates and describes many of the plants and animals that depend on the springs, rivers, beaches, marshes, and reefs in and around Florida, including corals, sharks, lobsters, alligators, manatees, birds, turtles, and fish. Suggests ways everyone can help protect Florida's priceless natural resources. Ages 10–14.